Orchard Books, 95 Madison Avenue, New York, NY 10016

Manufactured in Belgium
Book design by Jennifer Browne

10 9 8 7 6 5 4 3 2 1

The text of this book is set in Goudy Sans Medium.
The illustrations are alkyd paintings.

Library of Congress Cataloging-in-Publication Data
Verboven, Agnes.
[Alle eendjes zwemmen in het water. English]
Ducks like to swim / by Agnes Verboven ; pictures by Anne
Westerduin ; [translated by Dominic Barth]. — 1st American ed.
p. cm.
Summary: An assortment of animals join a mother duck in making
noises in an effort to bring on rain.
ISBN 0-531-30054-4
[1. Ducks—Fiction. 2. Animal sounds—Fiction.] I. Westerduin,
Anne, ill. II. Barth, Dominic. III. Title.
PZ7.V5825Du 1997 [E]—dc21 97-5038

AGNES VERBOVEN

Ducks Like
To Swim

Pictures by

ANNE WESTERDUIN

ORCHARD BOOKS

NEW YORK

Ducks like to swim.

One day there is not enough water.
Mother duck quacks for rain.

Quack! Quack!

Who will help?

Rooster crows.

Cock-a-doodle-doo!

Friendly dog barks.

Bowwow-wow!

Stripy cat meows.

Mee-oww-rrr!

Lazy cow moos.

Moo-oooo!

Brown horse neighs.

Neigh! Neigh!

Woolly sheep bleats.
Baa! Baa! Baa!

Curly-tailed pig squeals.

Oink! Oink!

Donkey brays.

Hee-haw!

All together now! Ready?

1, 2, 3 . . .

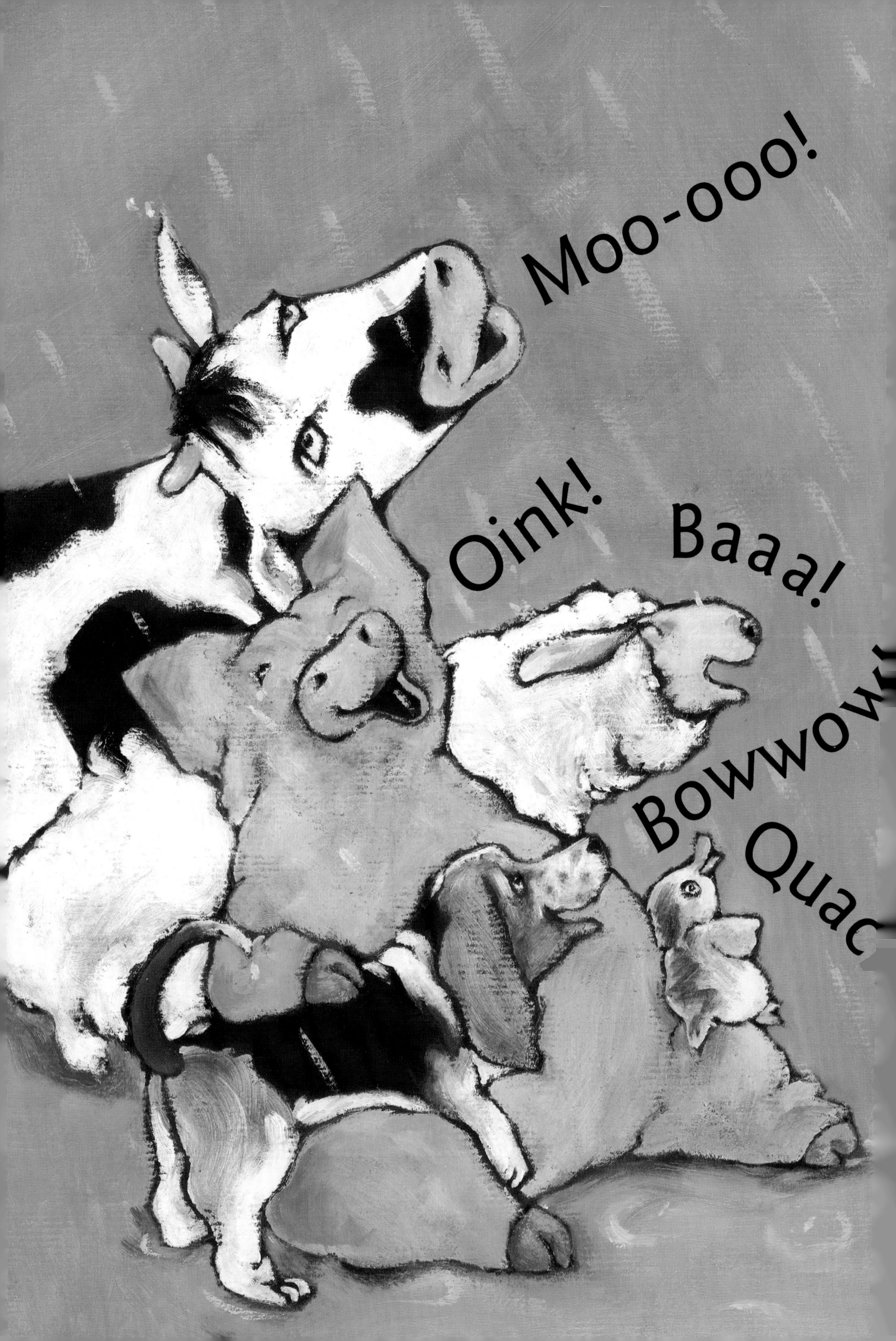
Moo-ooo!
Oink!
Baaa!
Bowwow
Quac

Quack! Quack!

Ducks like to swim.